CLASSIC ROCK BANDS

QUEEN

by Alexis Burling

CONTENT CONSULTANT

Daniel Nester
Associate Professor
Department of English
The College of Saint Rose

An Imprint of Abdo Publishing | abdobooks.com

abdobooks.com

Published by Abdo Publishing, a division of ABDO, PO Box 398166, Minneapolis, Minnesota 55439.

Printed in the United States of America, North Mankato, Minnesota.
052021
092021

Cover Photo: RB/Redferns/Getty Images
Interior Photos: Mike Cameron/Redferns/Getty Images, 4–5; Joe Schaber/AP Images, 8–9; PA Wire URN:13255889/Press Association/AP Images, 11; FG/Bauer-Griffin/Michael Ochs Archives/Getty Images, 14–15; Shutterstock Images, 16–17; Mark and Colleen Hayward/Redferns/Getty Images, 20–21; iStockphoto, 23; George Wilkes/Hulton Archive/Getty Images, 26; South Coast Press/Rex Features, 28–29, 38–39; Tracksimages.com/Alamy, 33; KW Photography/Alamy, 35; Monitor Picture Library/Photoshot/Hulton Archive/Getty Images, 41; Martyn Goddard/Alamy, 45; Andre Csillag/Rex Features, 49; Martyn Goddard/Corbis Premium Historical/Getty Images, 50–51; Legon/Rex Features, 53; Hulton Archive/Getty Images, 56–57; Richard E. Aaron/Redferns/Getty Images, 60–61; Stephen Chung/Alamy, 64; Ilpo Musto/Rex Features, 67, 68; Walter McBride/MediaPunch/IPX/AP Images, 70; Denis O'Regan/Premium Archive/Getty Images, 72–73; David Segal/AP Images, 74–75; Dave Hogan/Hulton Archive/Getty Images, 77; Alan Davidson/Rex Features, 80–81; Gill Allen/AP Images, 84, 86–87; Paramount/Photofest, 90–91; Featureflash Photo Agency/Shutterstock Images, 95; Balazs Mohai/EPA-EFE/Shutterstock, 96–97

Editor: Melissa York
Series Designer: Colleen McLaren

Library of Congress Control Number: 2019954390

Publisher's Cataloging-in-Publication Data

Names: Burling, Alexis, author.
Title: Queen / by Alexis Burling
Description: Minneapolis, Minnesota : Abdo Publishing, 2022 | Series: Classic rock bands | Includes online resources and index.
Identifiers: ISBN 9781532192029 (lib. bdg.) | ISBN 9781532179921 (ebook)
Subjects: LCSH: Queen (Musical group)--Juvenile literature. | Rock and roll bands--Biography--Juvenile literature. | Rock musicians--England--Biography--Juvenile literature. | Rock and roll music--Juvenile literature.
Classification: DDC 782.42166--dc23

CONTENTS

CHAPTER ONE

"The World's Greatest Rock Gig"

It was an event rock fans around the world had been eagerly anticipating for months. On July 13, 1985, a worldwide super concert was scheduled to take place at Wembley Stadium in London, England. Called Live Aid, the music festival had been organized to raise money for famine relief in the East African nation of Ethiopia. More than 75 musicians and bands planned to perform there and at JFK Stadium in Philadelphia, Pennsylvania, including Led Zeppelin, the Who, Black Sabbath, David Bowie, Elton John, and U2.[1] The concert would also be broadcast simultaneously on television so viewers at home could tune in.

Live Aid was one of the biggest rock music events of all time.

FEED THE WORLD
13th 1985 at WEMBLEY STADIUM
LIV
AID

If all went according to plan, it would be one of the biggest concerts in rock history.

Live Aid at JFK Stadium

Half of the live performances at Live Aid were held at Wembley Stadium in London, England. But a massive crowd of 100,000 people also gathered at JFK Stadium in Philadelphia, Pennsylvania, to watch the live television broadcast of the event.[3] Many musical acts also performed at JFK Stadium, including Bob Dylan, Eric Clapton, Mick Jagger, Madonna, and Tom Petty and the Heartbreakers.

However, one band felt ambivalent about taking part in the event. According to its front man, Freddie Mercury, Queen wasn't so sure the effort was worth it. The band included Mercury on lead vocals, piano, and guitar; Brian May on guitar and vocals; Roger Taylor on drums and vocals; and John Deacon on bass guitar. They had just completed their spring 1985 tour of New Zealand, Australia, and Japan, and they were mentally and physically exhausted. "We were all forming a sort of a rut," Mercury said at the time. "I wanted to get out of this last 10 years of what we were doing. It was so routine. It was like, go to the studio, do an album, go out on the road, go [around] the world and flog it to death, and by the time you came back it was time to do another album."[2]

Despite Mercury's misgivings, organizer Bob Geldof ultimately convinced the members of Queen to sign on. In preparation, the band created its ideal set list, which included "Bohemian Rhapsody," "Crazy Little Thing Called Love," "We Are the Champions," and more of its greatest hits. In the weeks before, they booked the 400-seat Shaw Theatre in London and spent hours practicing to get their timing right and their solos flawless. They also chose what they considered to be the most opportune time slot: 6:41 p.m., right at the beginning of prime-time television in the United Kingdom, when millions of people would be watching.

> "Fred, why wouldn't you do it? The entire stage was built for you, practically. Darling, the world."[4]
>
> *– Bob Geldof, Live Aid organizer, convincing Mercury to perform*

By the time Live Aid rolled around, Queen was prepared to play a fine set. Still, the band underestimated just how big and important the concert would be. For them, it was just another concert in a sea of many over a long, mostly successful career. But when the day finally arrived, no one—not even Geldof or the hundreds of thousands of fans who planned to watch the live concert on TV—had any idea that Mercury and the rest of Queen were about to make music history.

Giant crowds packed the stadium to see the greatest acts in the world perform.

A SHOWSTOPPING PERFORMANCE

On Saturday, July 13, Live Aid kicked off to an explosive start, with more than 70,000 screaming fans packed into Wembley Stadium.[5] Irish front man Bono and his band, U2, nailed their two-song set,

which ended with a 12-minute version of "Bad." In a duet with Sting, Dire Straits sang "Money for Nothing," one of the most popular hits of the summer. Later in the lineup, David Bowie wowed the crowd, as did the Who in their first performance in three years. Superstar Elton John took the

Mercury's Live Aid outfit has become iconic.

A Global Charity Event

The Live Aid music festival was organized in ten weeks. In addition to the live show performed in London and the simultaneous television broadcast at JFK Stadium in Philadelphia, the concert was broadcast on televisions in homes around the world. Thirteen satellites beamed the program to more than one billion viewers in more than 110 countries worldwide. More than 40 countries also ran telethons during the broadcast to raise money for famine relief in Africa. By the end of the event, more than $127 million had been raised.[7]

stage with special guest Wham!

But before Bowie and the rest performed, a band that many considered to be a wildcard prepared to take the spotlight. Just before seven o'clock, comedians Griff Rhys Jones and Mel Smith appeared on stage wearing police uniforms. They joked about receiving a noise complaint from a woman in Belgium but assured everyone the concert would continue as scheduled. Then they introduced the next act: "Her Majesty . . . Queen!"[6]

Wearing a low-cut white tank top and tight, white Wranglers with a black, studded belt and a similar armband around his right bicep, Freddie Mercury jogged onto the stage and sat down at his Steinway piano as the rest of Queen filed in. Looking out into the audience, the band played an abridged version of its 1975 hit "Bohemian Rhapsody," followed by

a medley of some of its greats, including "Radio Ga Ga"; its newest single, "Hammer to Fall"; the rockabilly "Crazy Little Thing Called Love"; and a drum-heavy "We Will Rock You." The audience stomped along to the beat.

Throughout the performance, Mercury danced and strutted around the stage like a possessed madman, wielding the sawed-off microphone like an air guitar. The only time he stopped moving was after "Radio Ga Ga." He stood at the front of the stage and led the fired-up audience in call-and-response, as they sang along to "Ay-oh." His final callout was later dubbed by music critics as "the note heard around the world."[8] At the end of the allotted 20 minutes, Queen finished with "We Are the Champions," and the cheering crowd went wild.

Loud and Proud

Queen's performance at Live Aid is widely acknowledged to be one of the greatest rock performances of all time. But in addition to Mercury's antics on stage and the rest of the band's flawless execution, something else contributed to the band's overwhelming success that night: volume. According to an interview with Taylor for *Mojo* magazine, Queen's engineer adjusted Wembley Stadium's sound system settings right before the band went on stage. In turning up the volume metaphorically but also literally, Queen's performance was louder and had a greater impact than everyone else's.

QUEEN STEALS THE SHOW

After Live Aid was over, it was clear that Queen had pulled off the tightest and most magnetic set of the evening. "Queen [was] absolutely the best band of the day. They played the best, had the best sound, used their time to the [fullest]," said Bob Geldof. "They understood the idea exactly, that it was a global jukebox. They just went and smashed one hit after another."[9]

The Ultimate Rock Star

After Queen played at Live Aid, many critics wrote that it was one of the most spectacular performances they had ever seen. Most attributed the success to Mercury. "He was a rock star playing a rock star, leather-lunged and imperious but also grinning to let everyone share the joke. And in Britain, where Queen had become a symbol of national pride, the Wembley crowd was his from the beginning, roaring back every call-and-response and doing a stadium-wide, hands-held-high double clap in 'Radio Ga Ga,'" wrote *New York Times* chief music critic Jon Pareles. "For 21 minutes, Freddie Mercury undeniably made the world his stadium."[10]

Even other performers like Elton John admitted that Mercury, Taylor, May, and Deacon had stolen the show. Perhaps Foo Fighters front man Dave Grohl best encapsulated what everyone was thinking then when he later talked about the event: "Queen smoked 'em. They just took everybody. They walked away being the greatest band you'd ever seen in your life, and it was unbelievable. And that's what made the band

Queen (*from left*, Deacon, Mercury, Taylor, May) takes a bow after one of the greatest sets in rock and roll history.

so great; that's why they should be recognized as one of the greatest rock bands of all time, because they could connect with an audience."[11]

Two months after Live Aid ended, Queen began working on a new studio album, their twelfth. After it was released, *A Kind of Magic* sold six million copies and was followed up with yet another world tour.[12]

Years later, Queen's Live Aid set is still seen as "the world's greatest rock gig," according to industry polls.[13] But the band wasn't always

considered the epitome of rock stardom. In fact, over the band's decades-long career, each of its members endured seemingly insurmountable setbacks—especially Mercury, who sadly died of complications from acquired immunodeficiency syndrome (AIDS) just a few years after the legendary Live Aid performance. Still, the legacy of Queen's music lives on.

> "I won't be a rock star. I will be a legend."[14]
>
> *– Freddie Mercury*

CHAPTER TWO

A Ragtag Group of London Musicians

According to the Rock & Roll Hall of Fame, "Queen was one of the most popular, ambitious, and beloved classic rock bands ever."[1] But like most music groups, its members didn't start out their careers knowing they were going to make chart-topping records, rake in millions of dollars, and change music history. Instead, for the first few years before they officially became known as Queen, two of Queen's founders, Brian May and Roger Taylor, were in another band altogether.

The seeds of Queen were planted during the mid-1960s. At the time, May was busy taking classes on astronomy, math, and

May and Taylor met and started playing together while May was studying at London's Imperial College.

physics at London's Imperial College. He was tall, rail thin, and soft spoken. Aside from studying, May spent most of his time listening to records by Buddy Holly and the Beatles and playing guitar in a cover band called 1984. Though 1984 did well enough playing songs written by groups such as the Shadows, the Yardbirds, and the Rolling Stones and even landed on the same bill as guitar legend Jimi Hendrix in 1967, May longed to get involved with musicians who actually wrote and played their own music.

In 1968, May left 1984 to start a new band with former 1984 bandmate Tim Staffell, who attended Ealing College and sang vocals. They called their group Smile. Because they didn't know any drummers talented enough to recreate the beats they hoped to emulate—like those of Cream's Ginger Baker or Mitch Mitchell, who played

The Legendary Red Special

Brian May was always musically inclined. As a teenager growing up in the Feltham, Middlesex section of London, he was inspired by the unique harmonies of Buddy Holly and the Crickets, the Beatles' catchy melodies, and even the layered strings of Italian composer Mantovani. But he was also a proficient engineer. In 1963, May and his father built an electric guitar from scratch. They used mahogany parts from a 200-year-old fireplace mantle in the neck. The whammy bar, used to make vibrato sounds, was made out of a metal piece from a bicycle luggage rack. May and his father nicknamed it the Red Special. It became the guitar May played for his entire career.

drums for the Jimi Hendrix Experience—the group posted a call for a drummer on the Imperial College bulletin board. London Hospital Medical College dentistry student Roger Taylor answered the ad. After a brief audition, he snagged the spot.

"I remember being flabbergasted when Roger set his kit up at Imperial College," May told *Mojo* magazine in 1999. "Just the sound of him tuning his drums was better than I'd heard from anyone before."[2]

Smile played gigs for most of 1968. The group jammed out to packed audiences throughout London and around England and developed quite a fan base. Young people, especially college students, loved following them around from venue to venue. One person in particular, a striking young

Roger Taylor's Musical Roots

From the time he was a little boy growing up in King's Lynn, Norfolk, and Cornwall, England, in the 1950s, Roger Taylor adored anything having to do with music. He learned to play the ukulele and was in a preteen skiffle band, though it only lasted for two gigs. In 1960, he taught himself to play guitar and sang in a church choir. Within a year, he had found his true calling: playing drums. In 1966, when he was still in high school, Taylor became the drummer and lead singer for Cornwall's most popular band, the Reaction. One thing in particular made the band unique. At most bands' gigs, the drum kit is set up toward the back of the stage. For the Reaction shows, Taylor's drum kit was always the focus of the show, front and center.

Smile—including May, *seated at rear in white jacket*, and Staffell, *third from right*—poses in London in 1969.

man with shaggy brown hair and soulful eyes named Farrokh Bulsara, became a devoted regular.

A FASHIONABLE ENTRANCE

Born on September 5, 1946, in Zanzibar, a British island protectorate off the east coast of Africa,

Farrokh "Freddie" Bulsara immigrated with his family to Feltham in Middlesex, England, in 1964. His father, Bomi, worked for the British government. His mother, Jer, and his father practiced Zoroastrianism, one of the world's oldest monotheistic religions. They were politically

Tourists still visit a house where Bulsara lived as a child in Stone Town, Zanzibar.

and morally conservative compared to London's freewheeling popular culture at the time, especially Bulsara's father. Though Freddie was close to his parents and sister, Kashmira, he spent a lot of time playing piano and listening to music in his room, including records by Little Richard, Fats Domino, and later the Beatles and the Rolling Stones. In 1966, he enrolled at Ealing College as an art student.

Though described by most of his classmates as shy and somewhat reserved in his early teens, Bulsara seemed to come into his own in college. With his long, brown hair, toothy smile, and magnetic features, he was renowned for wearing flamboyant clothing and painting his fingernails black. After befriending fellow Ealing College classmate Staffell,

Troublesome Teeth

In addition to his loud and flashy outfits, Bulsara was known for another exaggerated feature: his protruding teeth. Caused by four extra teeth at the back of his mouth pushing the front ones forward, his massive overbite could have triggered a number of serious health problems. Instead, it became one of his defining features and a calling card to stardom. Though Bulsara never opted for corrective surgery even after he and Queen became famous, his bucktoothed smile did embarrass him. "On screen he always covered his teeth with his top lip or raised his hand to cover them," said close friend and personal assistant Peter Freestone. "He was self-conscious about them."[3]

TEMBO HOUSE HOTEL
FREDDIE MERCURY
HOUSE
139
Venice Beach

Bulsara found a crew he felt at home with, one that included Taylor and May. When he graduated in 1969, he moved in with the members of Smile and started lobbying to become the group's lead singer.

In the meantime, Bulsara took a job at a Kensington clothing stall with Taylor to pay the bills and support his artist lifestyle. It was then that he met Mary Austin, a working-class woman who was 19 at the time—Bulsara was 24. She had briefly dated May in the past, and she worked at Biba, a high-end London shop where Bulsara would often go to dig up some of his outlandish outfits. Bulsara and Austin hit it off immediately. After a few months of dating, they moved into a cramped apartment. They bought secondhand furniture and started making a home together. Still, Bulsara never forgot about his plan to make music. As he was exploring what it meant to be in love for the first time in his life, he kept his watchful eye on Smile.

"The thing about Freddie was, he always had an unshakable faith in himself. People would say that he was shy, but deep down he had this absolutely unshakable faith. He used to say that he was gonna be a superstar someday."[4]

– Tim Staffell, speaking with Esquire *magazine in 2019*

DWINDLING SUCCESS

Despite Smile's initial success as a band, its track record was up and down throughout 1969. They recorded a single for Mercury Records, "Earth," in August of that year. Unfortunately, it didn't get much airtime and was considered a flop. That December, the band played a gig at London's prestigious Marquee Club. Not that many people showed up to see them play. Some of the people who did attend left before the set was over.

Freddie's Influences

During Bulsara's time in college, he sang the blues for a number of fledgling rock bands. Like many people at the time, he loved the Beatles and the Rolling Stones. But his musical influences extended beyond those of his bandmates. Among many others, they included British composer and singer Noël Coward, classical composers Frédéric Chopin and Wolfgang Amadeus Mozart, and contemporary stars Robert Plant of Led Zeppelin and Aretha Franklin. Bulsara also attributed many of his antics on stage to his two favorite stars, Jimi Hendrix and Liza Minnelli.

Early in 1970, Mercury Records dumped Smile for good. Staffell quit as well. According to later interviews, he thought the band just wasn't going anywhere and his musical interests were shifting toward jazz and blues. "I just said to them, 'Look guys, I've already gone for some auditions. . . . I'm

Bulsara always showed a flair for dramatic fashion.

not happy with this anymore and I don't think it's gonna work out,'" Staffell explained.[5]

Meanwhile, just as Smile was floundering and heading into a nosedive, Bulsara was busy flexing and stretching his own musical muscles, though without much success. First, he had a brief stint as the lead singer in a cover band called Wreckage. Then he joined another group called Sour Milk Sea. Neither band could attract a crowd, so both endeavors were short lived.

By mid-1970, Bulsara, Taylor, and May felt uncertain about their future as professional musicians. Yet despite their string of failures and lack of money, they couldn't fathom giving up their dream of becoming rock stars. Luckily for them, in just a few short months, their futures would align and take off in ways none of them could have imagined.

CHAPTER THREE

The Birth of Queen

After Tim Staffell left Smile, the band imploded. But despite its failure, Smile's original members remained friends. May and Taylor also yearned to create something new. Throughout Smile's run, Bulsara had urged them to form a different band, this time with him included. "If I was your singer, I'd show you how it was done," he'd often yell from the audience at a show.[1] The former Smile members realized it was time to take Bulsara up on his offer.

Queen's lineup was complete with the addition of Deacon, *left*, in 1971.

"The music scene in London in the '60s and '70s was really formed from the ground up. It was kids making it up in their garages, in their living rooms. . . . We had a big pool of musical friends that would combine and recombine, trying different band ideas out. It was like a melting pot."[2]

– Tim Staffell, 2019

In April 1970, May, Taylor, and Bulsara formed a trio and started looking for a bassist. They cycled through a few musicians during the first few months of playing gigs. Due to personality conflicts or musical differences, none of the bassists worked out for long.

Finally, in early 1971, the three bandmates met 19-year-old John Deacon at a London disco. At the time, he was studying for his master's degree in acoustics and vibration technology at Chelsea College, University of London. He was also a seasoned performer with a popular Leicestershire band called the Opposition. When May asked Deacon to audition, he was so shy and reserved that everyone was sure the arrangement would be another dud—until he picked up his bass. Deacon's playing was so tight and impressive that he was hired on the spot. The band's final lineup—May, Taylor, Bulsara, and Deacon—would last for the rest of the band's career.

WHAT'S IN A NAME?

Now that the new band was official, it needed a catchy name. The four members wanted it to be something young people would remember, like *the Beatles* or *the Rolling Stones*. May and Taylor suggested *the Rich Kids* and *the Grand Dance*, among dozens of other options.

Bulsara vetoed those options immediately, calling them unmemorable and boring. Instead, he insisted on the most eclectic and unforgettable name he could think of: *Queen*. "It's ever so regal. It was a strong name, very universal and very immediate," he said. "[The name *Queen*] had a lot of visual potential and was open to all sorts of

The Ace of Bass

John Deacon was born on August 19, 1951. When he was seven, his parents gave him a red plastic Tommy Steele guitar as a surprise. From the moment he picked up the instrument, he was hooked. As a teenager, Deacon saved up money from his newspaper delivery route to buy his first real guitar. Then at 14, he started the Opposition. They progressed from playing in his garage to drawing crowds in Leicestershire, England, Deacon's hometown.

In addition to playing the guitar, Deacon also excelled at the bass. That's the instrument he was playing when he first went to see May, Taylor, Bulsara, and a different bassist perform in October 1970. At the time, Deacon didn't think much of their show. "They were all dressed in black, and the lights were very dim too, so all I could see were four shadowy figures," he recalled in an interview. "They didn't make a lasting impression on me at the time."[3]

Changing his name was part of Mercury's transformation into a rock god.

interpretations, but that was just one facet of it."[4]

In addition to shaping the band's image, Bulsara longed to bust his own persona wide open. He dropped his last name and officially changed it to Mercury, after the Roman messenger of the gods. By changing his name, Freddie's transformation from wannabe unknown musician to larger-than-life singer destined for stardom was immediate, at least internally. "I think changing his name was part of him assuming this different skin," May said in a 2000 documentary. "I think it helped him to be this person that he wanted to be. The Bulsara person was still there, but for the public he was going to be this different character, this god."[5]

A Logo with Meaning

In addition to coming up with Queen's name, Mercury also designed and illustrated the band's logo, known as the Queen crest, in 1973. It loosely resembles England's royal coat of arms and combines the zodiac signs of Queen's four members: two lions for Deacon and Taylor (both Leos), a crab for May (a Cancer), and two fairies for Mercury (a Virgo). A phoenix, a mythical bird often used to represent rebirth and immortality, sits at the top center. According to the myth, the phoenix explodes into flames and then is reborn from the ash. "Freddie may be represented by the two fairies, but his life, work and incredible impact are destined to keep rising from the ashes," wrote music critic Stefan Kyriazis in 2019.[6]

Freddie Mercury's Complicated Sexuality

Throughout Queen's history as a band, Freddie Mercury was known for wearing unconventional clothing and makeup, especially for a man. Though he was dating Mary Austin during Queen's early years, he also never talked openly about his sexuality. This could be for a few different reasons. Mercury came of age during a time when same-sex attraction was considered a mental illness by some members of society. Gay and bisexual people were barely represented in the media, and most people believed being anything but heterosexual was unacceptable. In most US states and in the United Kingdom, having a sexual relationship with a member of the same sex was even considered illegal and therefore a crime. Mercury's parents also practiced Zoroastrianism, a religion that categorized homosexuality as a type of demon worship. Consequently, though Mercury had no qualms about flaunting his love of wearing fur, sequined bodysuits, tight pants, and nail polish, he mostly kept his sex life hidden.

SLOW BEGINNINGS

With its new name set and permanent lineup intact, Queen got down to business. Being in a rock band wasn't novel for Mercury, May, Taylor, or Deacon. But the process of putting out their first record was still slow going. For the first two years, they faced many problems and struggled to get off the ground. Aside from Mercury, Queen's three other members had academic careers that they hadn't given up on. May even kept working toward his PhD thesis in astrophysics when the band wasn't rehearsing. They worked at London's then new De Lane Lea recording studio and laid down tracks during

Producing Queen's first album took a lot of effort and persistence.

the studio's off time when other famous musicians weren't using the equipment. Some of Queen's bandmates suffered health issues during this time too. May nearly lost an arm to gangrene. The effect of all these obstacles was that the process of writing songs and recording them took longer than they expected.

Then, when Queen had cobbled together enough songs to put together a demo for potential record labels, the band fell victim to a few unsatisfactory business deals. First, they got a representation offer from Charisma Records, but they declined because the arrangement wasn't up to their standards. After more searching, they opted to go with Trident Studios, known for producing Lou Reed's *Transformer* and David Bowie's *Hunky Dory* and *The Rise and Fall of Ziggy Stardust and the Spiders from Mars*. Finally, two years after the band played its opening chord together, it recorded its first album in 1973. It was a mix of heavy metal, jam band riffs, and progressive rock, a genre that pushed the boundaries of rock and roll with unconventional ideas and sounds. The group called it *Queen*.

> "*Queen* is quite clearly the work of an assured group of young men. . . . A song like 'Son and Daughter' is like the lovechild of Black Sabbath and Ziggy Stardust, taking the most potent attributes of both, and refusing to tone down anything in favor of a harmonious mix. And they were just getting started."[7]
>
> – *Dominique Leone,* Pitchfork *(2011)*

Queen was released on July 13, 1973, by EMI Records in the United Kingdom and by Elektra Records in the United States. Mercury sang vocals and composed five of the ten tracks. Lead guitarist May composed four songs, including "Doing All Right," which he cowrote with Staffell. Taylor played drums, wrote, and sang lead vocals on "Modern Times Rock and Roll." The album's opening track was "Keep Yourself Alive," written by May. It was not a hit upon release, but it eventually became a popular song in their live performances.

Though it was the band's first release and was mostly praised by critics, *Queen* was received unenthusiastically by the public. Most people thought it was derivative of Led Zeppelin and David Bowie. In retrospect, the band's self-titled debut stands out as something that only scratched the surface of what was yet to come.

CHAPTER FOUR

Sheer Heart Attack

During the early 1970s, Freddie Mercury fully embraced his role as the front man of Queen. Wearing an angel-winged cloak or glittery pleather jumpsuit, mic stand in hand and strutting across the stage, he commanded the audience's attention every time the band played a show. But aside from performing in front of increasingly large crowds at venues around the United Kingdom and soon the United States, something else—something potentially life changing—was going on at home.

By 1973, Mercury and Austin had moved into a one-bedroom flat on London's Holland Road. According to the then 23-year-old

Mercury's early outfits, created by famous designer Zandra Rhodes, surprised and captivated audiences.

Poor Upbringings

Mary Austin was born in 1951 in South London's Battersea neighborhood. Her father had a job trimming wallpaper. Her mother was a domestic worker. Both of her parents were deaf, and the family was poor.

When Austin met Mercury, she immediately liked him. Still, she decided not to act overly smitten. When he asked her out on a date for his twenty-fourth birthday, she said she was busy. "I was trying to be cool," she recalled. "Not because there was any real reason I couldn't go. But Freddie wasn't put off. We went out the next day instead."[2]

Austin, she and Mercury were blissfully happy, though they never talked about their future. Then Christmas Day happened. When they exchanged gifts, Mercury gave Austin a big box. Nestled inside was a smaller box. Then another and another. Finally, Austin opened the last tiny box. Inside, she found a jade ring.

"I looked at it and was speechless. I remember thinking, 'I don't understand what's going on.' It wasn't what I'd expected at all," Austin said. "So, I asked him, 'Which hand should I put this on?' And he said, 'Ring finger, left hand.' And then he said, 'Because, will you marry me?' I was shocked. It just so wasn't what I was expecting. I just whispered, 'Yes. I will.'"[1]

Mercury beamed, overjoyed by her acceptance. He took Austin to meet his parents, who thought she was lovely. Though she was still shocked by Mercury's sudden proposal, Austin started to

Mary Austin, *left*, would stick by Mercury's side for the rest of his life.

plan for an eventual wedding. But as weeks, then months, passed and nothing happened, she started to worry.

"Sometime later, I spotted a wonderful antique wedding dress in a small shop. And as Freddie hadn't said anything more about marrying, the only way that I could test the water was to say, 'Is it time I bought the dress?' But he said no," Austin recalled in an interview. "I was disappointed but I had a feeling it wasn't going to happen. Things were getting very complicated and the atmosphere between us was changing a lot. I knew the writing was on the wall, but what writing? I wasn't absolutely sure."[3]

> "Mick Rock, the photographer, used to go around and have tea with [Mercury and Austin] and he said it would all be terribly sweet. The tablecloth would come out [along with] bone china cups and little teacups and nice little plates of biscuits. . . . They were [like] this old married couple."[4]
>
> *– Lesley-Ann Jones, author of* Bohemian Rhapsody: The Definitive Biography

ALBUMS APLENTY

Mercury and Austin would never end up getting married. But it wasn't because he had stopped loving Austin, at least as a person. One reason was that the band had just gotten busy. On March 8, 1974, Queen released its second album, *Queen II. Queen II* was full of intricate harmonies and Mercury's prominent piano solos, sounding more like progressive rock. Some of the 11 tracks had quirky names, such as "Ogre Battle" and "The Fairy Feller's Master-Stroke." The album wasn't well reviewed. May had to miss 41 shows on their *Queen II* spring tour throughout the United Kingdom and United States due to a bout of hepatitis. But the band was getting used to seeing more and more fans—including hordes of screaming girls—at its shows. Queen was also gaining confidence.

"We took so much trouble over that album, possibly too much, but when we finished, we felt really proud," Taylor later said of *Queen II*. "Immediately, it got really bad reviews so I took it home to listen to again and thought '[Are] they right?' But after hearing it a few weeks later, I still [liked] it. I [thought it was] great."[5]

On November 8, 1974, Queen released its third LP, *Sheer Heart Attack*, an album many critics and fans consider to be their breakout. "Killer Queen," the record's single, skyrocketed to Number 2 in the UK chart. It reached Number 12 on the *Billboard* chart in the United States—Queen's first appearance on the US Top 20. It was also the first time all four band members lent a hand in songwriting.

"With Queen, I have my favorite: *Queen II*. Whenever their newest record would come out and have all these other kinds of music on it, at first I'd only like this song or that song. But after a period of time listening to it, it would open my mind up to so many different styles. I really appreciate them for that."[6]

– Axl Rose, Guns N' Roses front man, speaking to Rolling Stone *magazine in 1989*

To promote *Sheer Heart Attack*, Queen embarked on its first headlining tour in the United Kingdom and the United States, also tacking on parts of Europe and Japan for the first time. They played more than 75 shows over the course of a few months. Audiences loved Mercury's soaring four-octave vocal range on "Lily of the Valley" and his thrash-metal style on "Stone Cold Crazy." Though the British press disagreed, fans couldn't get enough of Mercury's gaudy costumes. "*Sheer Heart Attack* proved that Queen was far from just any old rock band. This album took the band to a whole new level, helping to propel them from a support band on a US tour to a world headliner," wrote rock critic Max Bell.[7] But nothing could prepare the world for Queen's groundbreaking fourth album.

Bad Luck Streak

Recorded between July and September 1974 at four different studios, *Sheer Heart Attack* was produced fairly quickly. But it wasn't without setbacks. May caught an infection from an unclean needle during a routine vaccination in January 1974 in advance of the *Queen II* release. The resulting hepatitis flared up while they were working on the album, interrupting their spring tour. He recovered but was then hospitalized for a debilitating ulcer. Instead of dropping the ball altogether, Mercury, Taylor, and Deacon went into the recording studio anyway. When May felt well enough to play, he just laid his guitar solos and backup vocals over the recordings.

Queen played at home in London during the tour for *Sheer Heart Attack*.

"BOHEMIAN RHAPSODY"

By 1975, Queen had started recording its fourth album, *A Night at the Opera*. In September of that year, after an angry split with Trident Studios, the band negotiated itself out of its contract and searched for new management. After a few false starts, Queen hired British rock star Elton John's manager, John Reid.

For the album's single, Mercury had an idea for a song that would be something unlike anyone had ever heard before. He imagined a mix of vocals and instrumentals, with plenty of theatrics and soaring operatic overtones. He worked on the song day and night and enlisted the help of the rest of the band in spurts, along with producer Roy Thomas Baker. He wanted to call it "Bohemian Rhapsody."

During production, Queen overdubbed nearly 180 vocal tracks in order to create the song's now-famous cathedral-like chorus.[8] The band recorded one section of vocals, rewound the tape, then recorded more vocals on top of it, repeating the process numerous times. At one point, there were so many parts recorded on top of each other that the audiotape became

Say What?

Ever since it was recorded in 1975, "Bohemian Rhapsody" has befuddled fans and music critics alike, not only because of its far-out sound, but also because of its strange lyrics. Though Queen never fully revealed what everything in the song meant, here is a cheat sheet for some of its terms: Scaramouche is a fool-type character from the Italian clown tradition, called *commedia dell'arte*. A fandango is a Spanish flamenco dance. Galileo was an Italian astronomer who lived during the 1600s. He is often called the father of physics. Figaro is a character in Rossini's opera *The Barber of Seville*. "Bismillah" means "in the name of Allah" and is the first word in the Quran. "Mamma Mia!" is an Italian expression of surprise. It is also the title of an ABBA song that hit the top of the British charts right around the same time "Bohemian Rhapsody" did.

nearly translucent. If the band had done any more recording on that tape, it would have disintegrated.

Finally, "Bohemian Rhapsody" was finished and ready for release. But there was just one problem. At nearly six minutes, the song was too long to play on the radio. Reid insisted it wasn't commercial enough for the average listener. Instead, he thought it was way too wacky, even for 1970s audiences that liked experimental music. Deacon reluctantly agreed. But as with most decisions Queen had to make over the course of its career, Mercury had the final say: it was perfect and had to be released without any changes. May and Taylor agreed.

After the single hit the airwaves, "Bohemian Rhapsody" sold more than one million copies.[9] It became Queen's first Number 1 British single and stayed at the top spot for nine weeks. It also hit the Top 10 in the United States. Elated, Queen filmed a promotional video for the song, considered by many rock historians to be the world's first professional music video.

As of 2019, "Bohemian Rhapsody" was the third-best-selling single of all time in the United Kingdom. It was the only single ever to sell one million copies on two separate occasions.[10] It became the Christmas Number 1 twice in the United Kingdom, the only single ever to do so.

Queen at Rockfield Studios in Monmouth, Wales, where the band recorded "Bohemian Rhapsody"

A Night at the Opera was the band's first platinum album. It went triple platinum in the United States.

By the end of 1975, Queen had transformed into a true powerhouse band. The quartet was at the top of its game. Riding high and coming off the successes of "Bohemian Rhapsody" and yet another world tour, the four men went back into the studio to prepare for their fifth album. For Mercury and every member of the band, 1976 would be a year of stardom but also great change.

CHAPTER FIVE

Trouble in Paradise

After the huge triumph of "Bohemian Rhapsody" and the *A Night at the Opera* tour around the United Kingdom, the United States, Japan, and Australia, Queen entered a new, grander stage of stardom. Fans clamored to hear the band's music, and all four of Queen's albums hit the UK Top 20. Buoyed by this success, Queen went back into the studio to record its fifth album. The album's single—an operatic, Aretha Franklin–style song called "Somebody to Love"—featured many of the same layered vocals and sweeping instrumentals that worked so well in "Bohemian Rhapsody."

The checkered suit Mercury wore during the band's 1977 tour has become iconic.

"You can imagine how long it took to do ["Somebody to Love"]—over and over and over again. We spent a week on that, but it was worth it," Mercury said. "People probably think, 'Oh, God, they're in the studio again for four and a half months,' but we think it's necessary because it just has to be right, that's all."[1]

Queen Plays Hyde Park

In advance of *A Day at the Races*, Queen scheduled a four-day spree of summer concerts in the United Kingdom. On September 18, 1976, the band threw a free concert in London's Hyde Park. An estimated 150,000 to 200,000 people showed up to the event—a record for the park that still stands to this day.[2] The band opened with "Bohemian Rhapsody," with Mercury galloping onto the stage wearing an extravagant white jumpsuit. Later, he changed into a black leotard with a diamond-studded crotch. The fans went wild for the spectacle, cheering and making a ruckus. Because of all the noise, the police enforced a curfew before Queen had a chance to perform the encore. Mercury tried to go back on stage anyway, but the cops prevented him from doing so.

The album's opening track, May's "Tie Your Mother Down," was based on a piece he'd written while studying for his PhD in astronomy in 1968. The closing song, "Teo Torriatte (Let Us Cling Together)," was inspired by the band's tour stops in Japan and contained two entire verses written and sung in Japanese. Mercury's "You Take My Breath Away," featuring piano solos and more layered vocals, would become

Success and chart-topping music continued to roll in for Queen through the mid-1970s.

a popular sing-along at concerts in the months to come.

On December 10, 1976, *A Day at the Races* was released to the masses, just in time for Christmas. Once again, the album topped the charts, flying up to Number 1 in the United Kingdom and landing in the US Top 5. Advance orders alone totaled more than 500,000 copies.[3] Queen performed sold-out shows at Madison Square Garden, New York, in

"Of all the more theatrical rock performers, Freddie took it further than the rest. . . . He took it over the edge. And of course, I always admired a man who wears tights. I only saw him in concert once and as they say, he was definitely a man who could hold an audience in the palm of his hand."[4]

– David Bowie, as told to Rolling Stone *magazine, 1992*

February 1977, and Earl's Court, London, the following June. But though Queen had become a huge international phenomenon and Mercury was more famous than he ever imagined, his life was far from perfect.

AN AMICABLE BREAKUP

Since Mercury's proposal to Austin six years prior, the idea of getting married had fallen off his radar. Instead, Mercury had transformed from an attentive stay-at-home boyfriend to a man who was gone for months touring all over the world with the band. Austin had also noticed a change in Mercury's behavior since the time they had moved in together. When he wasn't busy touring, he stayed out late until the wee hours of the morning and often came home drunk. Suspecting he was having an affair with another woman, in mid-1976 Austin decided it was time to say something.

"Even if I didn't want to fully admit it, I had realized that something was going on," Austin told *OK!* magazine in 2000. "Although I didn't know what it was, I decided to discuss it with Freddie. I told him, 'Something is going on and I just feel like a noose around your neck. I think it's time for me to go.'"[5]

Mercury insisted nothing was wrong. For months, he avoided confrontation and continued to come home after Austin had gone to bed. But eventually, their standoff hit a breaking point. He needed to come clean about what had been going on in his mind since his rise to fame. After a few failed attempts at trying to explain, Mercury confessed he thought he was bisexual.

What Is True Love?

During the tail end of Mercury's relationship with Austin and long after they had broken up, Mercury had flings and relationships with men. Still, despite not being romantically involved with her, Mercury still considered Austin to be his first true love. "All my lovers asked me why they couldn't replace Mary, but it's simply impossible," Mercury said in a 1985 interview. "The only friend I've got is Mary, and I don't want anybody else. To me, she was my common-law wife. To me, it was a marriage. We believe in each other, that's enough for me."[6]

For Austin, that level of attachment also proved to be difficult at times, especially in her new relationships. Each boyfriend had to contend with the other man in Austin's life, Freddie Mercury. All of them eventually decided they weren't up for the challenge, including Austin's ex-husband, Nick Holford, and the father of her two children, Piers Cameron.

Mercury led the rock star life, including at a 1977 party with fellow rock star Elton John, *left*, and longtime friend actor/singer Peter Straker, *center*.

"I'll never forget that moment," Austin said. "Being a bit naive, it had taken me a while to realize the truth. [After we talked,] he felt good about having finally told me he was bisexual. [But] I do remember saying to him at the time, 'No Freddie, I don't think you are bisexual. I think you are gay.'"[7]

After their discussion toward the end of 1976, Mercury and Austin decided to break up—at least romantically—for good. Still emotionally close, they continued living together for a time, throwing parties and respecting each other's boundaries. But eventually the constant partying got to be too much for Austin, and she moved out in 1977. Mercury's music publishing company bought her a flat nearby, so close that she could see his apartment from her bathroom window. Though they never got back together as a couple, Austin continued to go on tour with the band and remained close with Mercury for the rest of his life.

PARTY HEARTY

Now that Mercury was unattached romantically, he fully embraced his newfound position as a single man in the spotlight. He threw lavish parties that stretched until all hours of the night, sometimes lasting for days. People often dressed up, did a lot of drugs, and had sex with other partygoers, some of it unprotected. During the late 1970s and early 1980s, Mercury went through a string of boyfriends, including a short relationship with his personal manager, Paul Prenter.

> "I think Freddie reached a stage where he thought he was invincible. He convinced himself he was having a good time and maybe, in part, he was. But I think in part he wasn't."[8]
>
> *– Mary Austin, 2013*

The other members of Queen noticed Mercury's fast slide into excess. But though they were worried about his drug use and didn't approve of his failure to use protection when having sex, none of them ever distanced themselves from him for embracing his sexuality. In fact, they went beyond merely quietly supporting him, refusing to say anything about his private life to the media. For the rest of his life and Queen's career as a band, Mercury's sexuality was deemed his own business and kept off-limits for comment by all members of the band. For Queen, music was king.

Mercury and the Media

Throughout Queen's career, the media often wrote stories about its albums, the band members' solo careers, and their front man's zany, ever-changing wardrobe. But one thing that was rarely discussed was the nature of Mercury's sexuality. While most reporters assumed he was heterosexual while living with Austin, then gay in his later years, none of them could ever get Mercury to reveal his preference for women or men—or both. Over time, the mystery has prevailed. "When all is said and done, maybe what makes Freddie Mercury one of the most fascinating musicians of all time is that while his queerness cannot be denied, it will always be shrouded in his own distinct mystique," wrote *Billboard* magazine rock critic Stephen Daw in 2018.[9]

CHAPTER SIX

"We Will Rock You"

On December 2, 1977, a frenzied crowd filled the 20,000-seat Madison Square Garden in New York City.[1] They were there to see Queen perform. A half hour after the concert was supposed to begin, the band still hadn't appeared on stage. Suddenly at 8:45 p.m., two telltale drumbeats reverberated around the stadium, followed by a tap of Roger Taylor's drumsticks. Boom, boom, tap. Boom, boom, tap.

The audience went wild, stomping their feet and clapping in time to the beat. Then a spotlight shone on Mercury as he began to sing. "Everyone was screaming and clapping," said 17-year-old Colleen Hershon.

Queen played several successful concerts at Madison Square Garden in 1977 and 1978.

"I lost my breath. I grabbed [my friend] Lorraine's arm, and she grabbed mine. We both screamed in disbelief! I COULD NOT BELIEVE IT!"[2]

When "We Will Rock You" concluded, Hershon and the rest of Queen's fans jumped to their feet and yelled as loud as they could. By the end of the concert, the band had performed "Love of My Life," "I'm in Love with My Car," a new rock anthem called "We Are the Champions," and of course the legendary "Bohemian Rhapsody." For many of the songs, most of the crowd stayed standing. "It was the best $8.50 that I EVER spent!! It was the BEST Friday night I ever had!! Everyone lit matches and the Garden looked like a Christmas tree! I will always remember the first time that I saw Queen," Hershon said.[3]

> "Both ["We Are the Champions" and "We Will Rock You"] are not just a permanent part of the rock lexicon, but pump-up anthems that are still played on an almost-daily basis on radio and at just about every major sporting event on the planet—transcending time, fashion and their own seeming obstacles to popularity."[4]
>
> *– Gil Kaufman, Billboard.com*

For Queen's legions of fans, that concert at Madison Square Garden in support of the band's sixth album, *News of the World*, was truly a night to cherish. For Mercury, May, Taylor, and Deacon, the energy and ecstatic feedback they received from the audience during the sing-alongs was symbolic of what the group had become. Queen was no longer a band that played a good, sometimes great rock show at a medium-sized venue. It had transformed into a bona fide phenomenon that continuously booked sold-out shows at huge stadiums across the United States, the United Kingdom, and the world.

"We Are the Champions"

After *News of the World* was released on October 28, 1977, one of the album's hit singles—Mercury's "We Are the Champions"—was played on radio stations across Europe, the United Kingdom, and the United States. It reached Number 2 in the UK singles charts and Number 4 on the *Billboard* Hot 100 in the United States. The song went on to become one of Queen's most popular ever. In fact, in 2011, a team of scientists crowned it the catchiest in the history of pop music because it's so easy to join in and sing along.

"Every musical hit is reliant on [math,] science, engineering, and technology; from the physics and frequencies of sound that determine pitch and harmony, to the hi-tech digital processors and synthesizers which can add effects to make a song catchier," said Dr. Daniel Mullensiefen. "We discovered that there's a science behind the sing-along and a special combination of neuroscience, math and cognitive psychology that can produce the elusive elixir of the perfect sing-along song."[5]

NONSTOP TOURING

Over the next decade, Queen went from being the biggest band in Europe to the biggest band in the world.

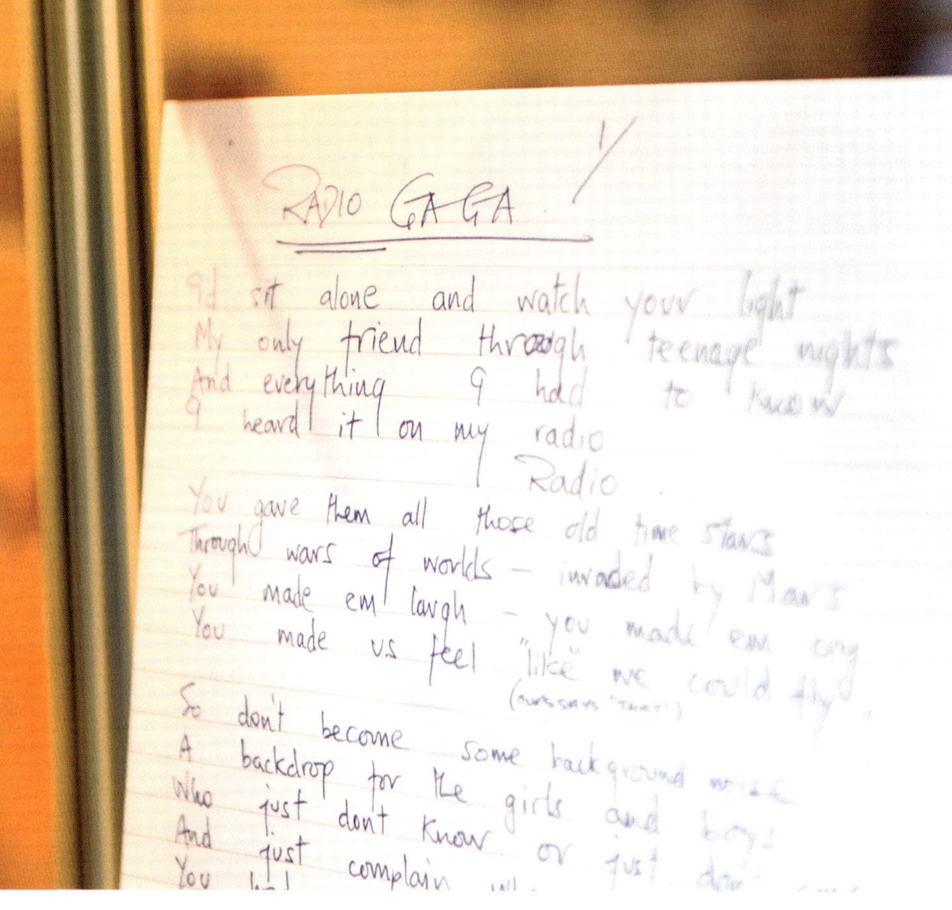

Taylor wrote the lyrics to "Radio Ga Ga" on a sheet of notebook paper.

It produced six more studio albums, including *Jazz* (1978), *The Game* (1980), *Flash Gordon* (1980), *Hot Space* (1982), *The Works* (1984), and *A Kind of Magic* (1986), with huge hits such as "I Want to Break Free" and "Radio Ga Ga." Queen also released a number of live albums, including *Live Killers* (1979) and *Live Magic* (1986). By the end of 1980 alone, it had sold more than 45 million albums worldwide and showed no signs of slowing down anytime soon.[6]

To make the most of their album releases and their era-defining pop-rock sound, the band embarked on increasingly lengthy tours. Their stadium performances were not just concerts but full-blown technical extravaganzas, with light shows, explosive sound, and of course Mercury's ever-evolving wardrobe changes. Starting in the late 1970s, Mercury often appeared on stage wearing full leather outfits or tight shorts and a tank top. This trimmed-down image reflected not only Queen's shift away from hard rock toward a more danceable New Wave, keyboard-dominated sound, but perhaps Mercury's personal

The Game: A Record Packed with Hits

In 1979, Queen relocated to Munich, Germany, for the summer to produce a new album. When it was released on June 30, 1980, *The Game* was a massive success. It marked Queen's commercial peak in the United States. Two of the album's major songs—"Crazy Little Thing Called Love" and "Another One Bites the Dust"—have amusing origin stories. Inspired by rock and roll star Elvis Presley, "Crazy Little Thing Called Love" was written in under ten minutes by Mercury in the bathtub. The song became the band's first Number 1 *Billboard* Hot 100 single in the United States.

Written by John Deacon, "Another One Bites the Dust" was inspired by the song "Good Times" by the disco group Chic. It became a hit thanks to pop legend Michael Jackson. According to Deacon, Jackson came backstage after a Queen concert and suggested the song be released as a single. The band was skeptical. But Jackson was right. It became the band's second US Number 1 hit.

Mercury cut his hair short in the late 1970s and added the mustache in the early 1980s.

style as well. His now short, slicked-back hair and trademark bushy mustache represented a style often seen in many gay clubs at the time, especially in Europe and the United States.

"Freddie loved the attention he and the band got in Argentina, especially from the local police—the band were always surrounded by motorcades, and smuggled in and out of gigs in armored vehicles. All that attention became a talking piece for Freddie, that would later always be brought up in conversation. It was, after all, history in the making."[9]

– Peter "Phoebe" Freestone, Mercury's personal assistant

In addition to spending more time on the road, Queen broke new ground by playing in previously uncharted markets. In 1981, the group toured the Far East and became the first band ever to schedule a stadium tour in countries south of the United States, hitting Argentina, Brazil, Venezuela, and Mexico. They performed in front of more than 250,000 people in São Paulo, Brazil—the largest paying audience for any band anywhere in the world at the time.[7] In 1986, Queen also played to a crowd of 80,000 in Budapest, Hungary.[8] It was one of the biggest rock concerts ever held in Eastern Europe during the years of communism.

But the world tours were not without obstacles.

Queen toured far and wide during the 1980s, including in Stockholm, Sweden, in 1985.

In 1981, Queen played a concert in Buenos Aires, Argentina's capital city. More than 300,000 people showed up to see the show—the country's largest concert at the time.[10] But fans elsewhere blasted the band for booking gigs in a country run by a ruthless right-wing military dictatorship rumored to have killed at least 30,000 citizens who disobeyed its rules.[11]

In October 1984, Queen was invited to do a 12-night run of concerts in Bophuthatswana, South Africa, at the Sun City Superbowl. Because the area was governed by the laws of apartheid, a strict system of racial segregation and discrimination, the United Nations had asked entertainers to boycott the country. Instead of bowing out of the engagement, Queen performed in South Africa anyway. Once again, critics and fans denounced that decision. As a result, Queen wasn't invited to participate with Band Aid, a collaboration between top British acts, to record "Do They Know It's Christmas?" to raise money to alleviate famine in Ethiopia.

SOLO CAREERS

For the final ten years of its touring era, Queen traveled far and wide. But though they were as tight as ever as a band, some members of the group also explored careers as solo musicians. In 1981,

In the early 1980s, Taylor began releasing solo albums while still remaining active in Queen.

Taylor released *Fun in Space*, followed by *Strange Frontier* in 1984. In 1987, he formed a band called the Cross, singing lead vocals and playing rhythm guitar. The Cross released three albums before disbanding in 1993.

Though Deacon didn't branch out to produce his own album during this time, he did sub in for different bands when Queen wasn't in the recording studio or out on tour. He released the single "Picking Up Sounds" as one-half of the duo Man Friday & Jive Junior, and he frequently played with the band the Immortals. Deacon also collaborated with Elton John from time to time and was part of the soundtrack to the 1988 film *Biggles: Adventures in Time*.

Perhaps the most prominent side projects were Mercury's. In 1985, when he was under the influence of his personal manager, Paul Prenter, he recorded his first solo album, *Mr. Bad Guy*. Though Mercury was quite proud of his compilation of power ballads and disco-infused songs, the record didn't do as well as he had hoped. It reached Number 6 in the United Kingdom and only Number 159 on the US charts. In 1988, he and one of his longtime idols, operatic soprano Montserrat Caballé, teamed up on Mercury's second solo album, *Barcelona*. Full of classical duets with operatic overtones, the record was famously cited by critics as being "one of the most confusing albums ever created."[12]

A Bad Influence

From 1977 to 1986, Paul Prenter served as Mercury's personal manager. The two were also intimately involved for a time. Due to Prenter's subtle control over Mercury and Queen's sound, May and Taylor have since referred to him in articles as a bad influence. After the band fired Prenter in 1986, he leaked information about Mercury to British tabloid the *Sun*. In the article, Prenter spilled details about Mercury's sex life, claiming Mercury had slept with hundreds of men. Prenter also told the world that Mercury had been tested for the human immunodeficiency virus (HIV).

By the mid-1980s, the members of Queen—as a band and in their solo ventures—were starting

Queen's helicopter flew over the massive crowd to bring the rock group to its final concert.

to come down off the incredible high of recording albums, touring, and living sporadically in New York, the United Kingdom, and Munich, Germany. Emotionally and physically exhausted, the band collectively decided to take a break from doing any major shows, aside from its groundbreaking set at the Live Aid concert in 1985. Mercury's final live performance with Queen took place on August 9, 1986, at Knebworth Park in Knebworth, England.

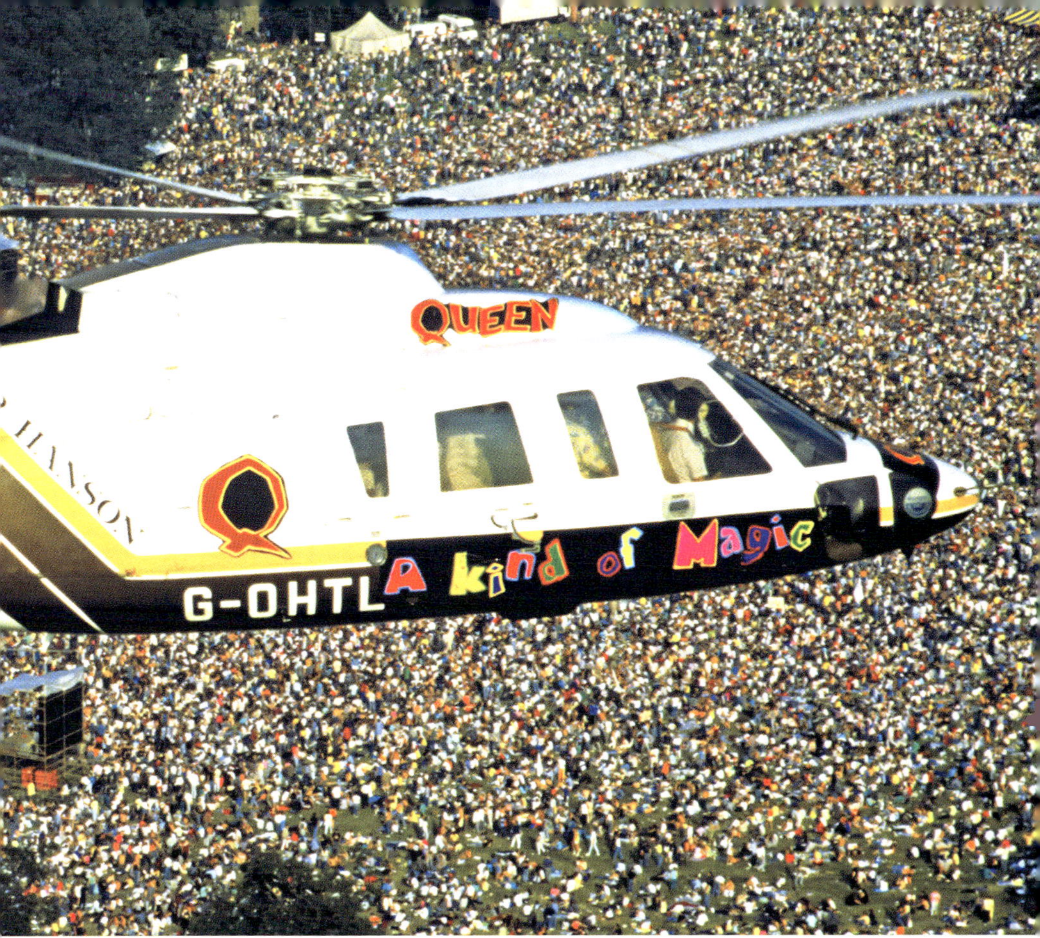

At least 160,000 people attended.[13] Queen arrived by helicopter.

For the incredibly emotional finale, Queen's rendition of the British national anthem, "God Save the Queen," reverberated through the crowd. Mercury wore a luxurious, flowing velvet robe. As he lifted a vibrant, bejeweled golden crown high in the sky and looked out at his adoring fans, he bid a solemn farewell to the crowd. No one knew at the time that it would be his final public performance.

CHAPTER SEVEN

The Loss of a Rock Icon

In the early 1980s, people all over the United States were worried about a new illness sweeping the country. They were especially concerned in New York, where about one-half of the infections were first recorded. The disease was called AIDS. Scientists soon learned it was caused by HIV, a debilitating virus that weakened the immune system. At that time, AIDS was nearly always fatal.

In its early years, especially before the general public knew much about HIV and AIDS, people called it the "gay plague" or "gay cancer" because it seemed to be spreading rapidly among gay men

A crowd marches to remember people who died from AIDS. Mercury was one of the first major celebrities to fatally contract the virus.

Being
Alive
Being
Alive

in particular. But although it hit the gay community the hardest during the 1980s, the disease doesn't actually discriminate. It's transmitted by infected bodily fluids, including semen and blood. The illness is mainly spread by drug users who share hypodermic needles and by infected people who have unprotected sex.

For years, Mercury's sexuality was called into question by members of the media and even by Queen's fans. By the mid-1980s, he had had dozens of romantic partners. He eventually settled into a seven-year relationship with Irish-born hairdresser Jim Hutton. Still, Mercury was renowned for his carefree attitude in matters related to sex. Because of this and despite his repeated denial whenever the topic came up, many people speculated that Mercury might be infected with HIV.

"It may not seem so long ago, but in terms of attitudes and prejudice it was a markedly different era, with severe stigma around both being an out celebrity (and the impact that could have on a career) and being HIV-positive."[1]

– *Tim Teeman,* Daily Beast

AN HIV DIAGNOSIS

By late 1985, Queen was in between albums and Mercury had grown tired of the club scene in Munich and New York. He returned home to London

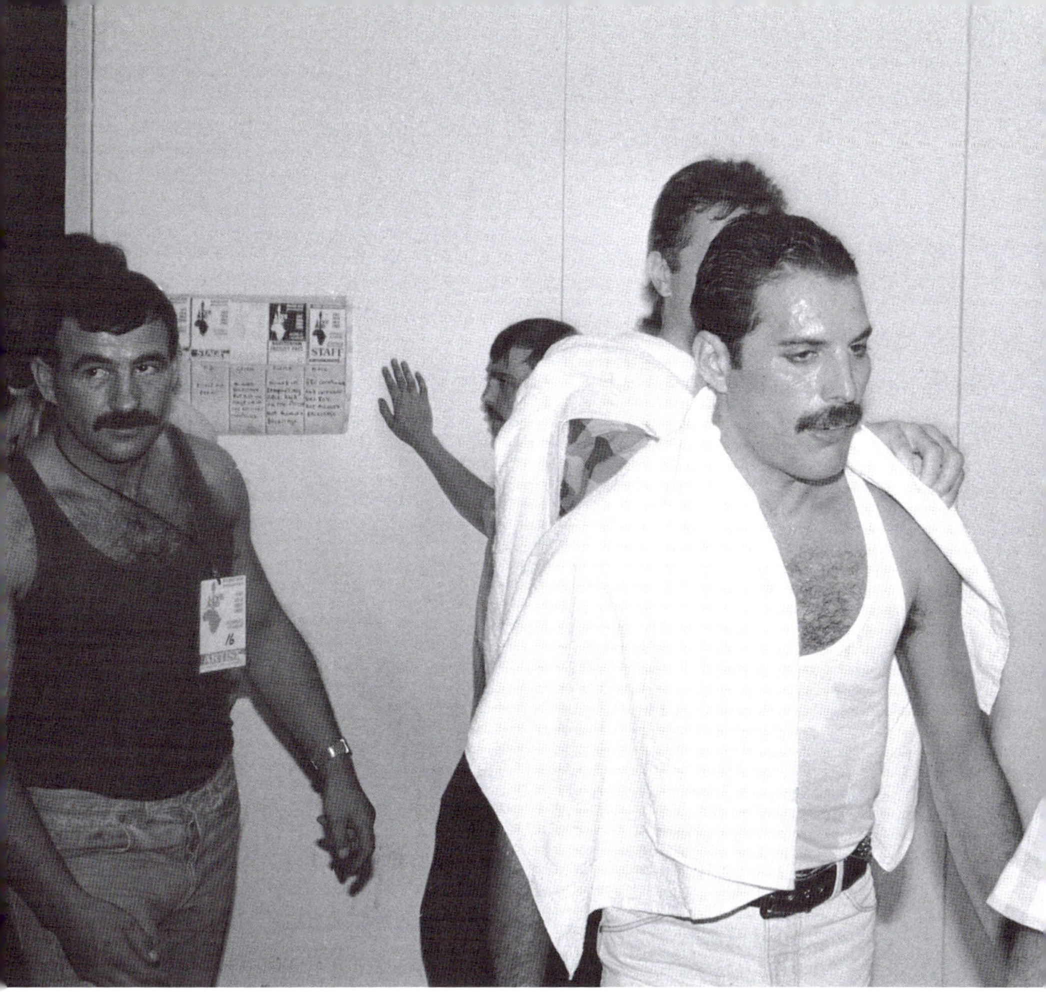

Mercury with his partner Jim Hutton, *far left*, backstage after his performance at Live Aid

and began spending more time with Hutton. Mercury also secretly got an HIV test. The results were negative, but he wouldn't stay disease-free for long.

Two years later, in 1987, Mercury found a strange lump on his shoulder. Again, he went to get tested. Though the doctor called Mercury repeatedly, he never returned to pick up the results. Finally, the doctor contacted Austin, who was now Mercury's secretary, to deliver the news. Mercury was HIV positive. "I felt my heart fall," Austin said later.[2]

Mercury started taking azidothymidine (AZT) and every other HIV-related drug available. A legion of doctors came to his Kensington mansion to treat him, but nothing seemed to help. Yet despite mounting suspicion by the public and members of the press because of his increasingly gaunt appearance, Mercury continued to deny he was infected with the virus—even to members of his band.

The turning point came in 1989, just after Queen released its thirteenth album, *The Miracle*. Usually after releasing an album, the

A Match for the Ages

Mercury and Hutton were romantically involved for seven years. Mercury met Hutton at a gay nightclub in London in 1985. At the time, Hutton had no idea who Mercury was. But less than a year after they started dating, Hutton moved into Mercury's Kensington home.

The two loved each other deeply, but their relationship wasn't perfect. Mercury never publicly came out, but that didn't bother Hutton. What did make him jealous was Mercury's habit of flirting with other men. "One day I saw him leaving his Kensington flat with another guy and we had an argument," Hutton told the *Times of London*. "I told him he had to make his mind up."

The ultimatum did it. Eventually Mercury toned down his promiscuity. "He said, 'OK,' he wanted to be with me. Deep down I think that he wanted to be secure with someone who was down to earth and not impressed by who he was," Hutton said.[3]

band picked out its tour stops, relished its bump in popularity, and had a bit of fun after doing so much work. This time, Mercury insisted on jumping right back into the studio to record another album. But first, he called his bandmates over to his house for a meeting.

"You probably realize what my problem is," Mercury told them. "Well, that's it and I don't want it to make a difference. I don't want it to be known. I don't want to talk about it. I just want to get on and work until I [drop]. I'd like you to support me in this."[4]

Mercury's bandmates were devastated. But there was nothing to be done. "We all went off and got quietly sick somewhere, and that

Treatment for AIDS

Thanks to advances in medicine, people who are infected with HIV today have a lot more options when it comes to treatment, including an array of drugs that help lower the viral load and fight infection. Those infected can live for many years, or even an entire average life span, taking drugs that prevent AIDS from taking over their bodies. In fact, there were approximately 1.1 million diagnosed and undiagnosed people living with HIV in the United States at the end of 2015, according to the most recent figures from the Centers for Disease Control and Prevention. Fifty-one percent of them were able to bring the amount of the virus in their bodies down almost to nothing.[5] But during the 1980s when Mercury got infected, the outcome wasn't so positive. At the time, only one drug, AZT, was available, and it wasn't that effective on its own. Nearly everyone who contracted HIV died from AIDS or related complications.

Queen together publicly for the last time on the night of the Brit Awards, 1990

was the only conversation directly we had about it," May said.[6]

THE WORLD GRIEVES

Not even a year after Mercury first informed his bandmates about his illness, his health began declining rapidly. He rarely appeared in public, instead preferring to stay home with Hutton, his cats, or Austin by his side. On February 18, 1990,

he made his final major public appearance at the Brit Awards held at the Dominion Theatre in London. Emaciated and with thinning hair, he joined the rest of Queen to collect the Brit Award for Outstanding Contribution to British Music.

Despite concerns from his bandmates who perpetually worried about his physical health and increasingly depressed mental state, Mercury insisted on finishing up what he knew would be his final album. Queen traveled to Montreux, Switzerland, to record in the studio there, far away from the prying press. "We all knew there wasn't much time left," May said. "Freddie wanted his life to be as normal as possible. He obviously was in a lot of pain and discomfort. [But] for him the studio was an oasis, a place where life was just the same as it always had been. He loved making music, he lived for it."[7]

> "This is hard to explain to people, but it wasn't sad, it was very happy. He was one of the funniest people I ever encountered. I was laughing most of the time, with him. Freddie was saying [of his illness], '[Screw] that. I'm not going to think about it, I'm going to do this.' We all were."[8]
>
> *– Justin Shirley-Smith, assistant studio manager at Montreux*

Innuendo, Queen's final album as a foursome, was released on February 5, 1991. Full of meaningful lyrics and gorgeous, sweeping melodies, it was the band's way of putting into words what Mercury could no longer express. "I think Roger and I kind of vocalized for him, in writing some of the lyrics. Because he was almost beyond the point where he could put it into words," May said. "So, songs like 'The Show Must Go On,' in my case, or 'Days of Our Lives,' in Roger's case, were things that we gave to Freddie as a way of him working through stuff with us. And that wasn't spoken. It was us trying to find the end before we got there."[9]

Though Queen fans adored the album and pleaded for the band to do a few shows, even just in London, Mercury was too sick to leave his bed. On November 23, 1991, Mercury issued a statement to the world:

> *Following enormous conjecture in the press, I wish to confirm that I have been tested HIV-positive and have AIDS. I felt it correct to keep this information private in order to protect the privacy of those around me. However, the time has come now for my friends and fans around the world to know the truth and I hope that everyone will join with me, my doctors and all those worldwide in the fight against this terrible disease. My privacy has always been very special to me and I am famous for my lack of interviews. Please understand this policy will continue.*[10]

"The album comes off as the work of an artist staring sickness right in the eye and vowing to "keep working until I . . . drop," as Mercury was once quoted as saying."[11]

Ron Hart, Rolling Stone *magazine, on* Innuendo

The next day, Mercury died. He was only 45 years old.

1 LOGAN PLA
GARDEN LOD

Fans left flowers outside Mercury's London house after his death.

On November 27, a small funeral was held at a church in London and attended by close friends and family. The ceremony was conducted by Zoroastrian priests. A recording by Aretha Franklin was played, as well as an aria performed by soprano Montserrat Caballé. The world had lost one of its most beloved rock icons. But though Mercury was gone, his legend—and Queen's long-lasting impact on music and fans—would live on.

Ashes Unknown

When Mercury died, he left most of his estate to Austin, including his mansion in Kensington and most of his multimillion-pound fortune. She also has an income for life from Mercury's portion of Queen's record sales. Austin still lived in the mansion as of 2019. "As much as I'd been a friend to him, I realized how much of a friend he'd been to me as well. He was always very protective of me. I only realized, after he died, quite how protective he'd been," she told *OK!* magazine.[12]

To return the favor, Austin took control of Mercury's ashes after he was cremated. After two years, she disposed of them in an undisclosed location. At his request, she has never revealed where she put them, not even to Mercury's family or his former bandmates. "I never betrayed Freddie in his lifetime. And I'll never betray him now," she said.[13]

CHAPTER EIGHT

Queen's Legacy

In the months following Mercury's death, the rest of Queen had a difficult time moving forward. In order to process some of their grief and celebrate their glorious front man's life in a way he would approve of, May, Taylor, and Deacon planned a tribute concert at London's Wembley Stadium. Within just a few hours and before the rest of the concert lineup was announced, the 72,000 allotted tickets were sold out.[1]

On April 20, 1992, the concert went off without a hitch. David Bowie sang "Under Pressure" with Annie Lennox. Elton John and Guns N' Roses front man Axl Rose performed "Bohemian Rhapsody." Even Liza Minnelli

May performed "Somebody to Love" at the Freddie Mercury tribute concert.

wowed the crowd with her rendition of "We Are the Champions." Perhaps the most showstopping moment was George Michael singing "Somebody to Love." "It was probably the proudest moment of my career, because it was me living out a childhood fantasy: to sing one of Freddie's songs in front of 80,000 people," Michael later said.[2]

The show was broadcast in 76 countries. More than one billion people tuned in around the world to watch the concert live.[3] As of 2019, the Freddie Mercury Tribute Concert for AIDS Awareness was still the largest performance held in tribute to a deceased musician.

After the groundbreaking concert, Queen disbanded for 13 years. Deacon retired

AIDS Awareness

After the Freddie Mercury Tribute Concert, May, Taylor, and Queen's manager, Jim Beach, used the proceeds from ticket sales to set up an AIDS awareness charity organization, the Mercury Phoenix Trust. The trust raises and donates money to small grassroots organizations around the world working to educate people about HIV/AIDS prevention. Since its founding in 1992, it has raised $15 million and funded more than 700 projects in 57 countries.[4]

In 2010, the Mercury Phoenix Trust launched the Freddie for a Day initiative. Every year on September 5, Mercury's birthday, fans get together and dress up like the beloved Queen front man to raise money. One year, a flash mob of bushy-mustachioed commuters took over Shimbashi Station in Tokyo, Japan.

from everything Queen related. Taylor continued his solo career, producing five more albums, from 1994's *Happiness?* to 2009's *The Unblinking Eye*. In 2007, May returned to Imperial College in London to complete his doctoral thesis in astrophysics, while still continuing to play music. His solo career included albums such as *Back to the Light* (1992) and *Another World* (1998). In 2015, he was ranked Number 26 on *Rolling Stone*'s list of the "100 Greatest Guitarists of All Time."

In 1995, a posthumous album of some of the unfinished songs Mercury was working on right before he died was released. With emotionally driven tracks about death, impermanence, love, and loss, the gorgeous *Made in Heaven* became one of Queen's top-selling albums. In one song, "Mother Love," May's voice takes over where Mercury's left off. "I can't take it if you see me cry. I long for peace before I die," Mercury sings. Then May continues, "My

> "I have never got over his death. None of us have. I think that we all thought that we could come to terms with it quite quickly, but we underestimated the impact his death had on our lives. I still find it difficult to talk about. For those of us left, it is as though Queen was another lifetime entirely."[5]
>
> *– Roger Taylor*

Wayne's World's Wayne and Garth famously headbanged to "Bohemian Rhapsody" in their car.

body's aching but I can't sleep, I'm coming home to my sweet mother love."[6]

THE BAND LIVES ON

Since Mercury's death and the band's long hiatus from recording, millions of Queen fans all over the world have grieved the loss of one of the most famous rock legends in music history. But a number of projects have kept the band's music in the

spotlight anyway. In 1992, "Bohemian Rhapsody" was used in the runaway hit comedy *Wayne's World*, starring Dana Carvey and Mike Myers. After the movie's release, the song reentered the US singles charts and shot up to Number 2 on the US *Billboard* Hot 100.

In 1997, a ballet by famous French choreographer Maurice Béjart using Queen's music premiered at the National Theatre in Paris. Five

A *Wayne's World* Phenomenon

In February 1992, a comedy movie called *Wayne's World* came out in theaters. It was based on a skit from the TV show *Saturday Night Live* about Wayne and Garth, two rock-obsessed hosts of a public access program. In one memorable scene, Wayne and Garth are driving around in an old, beat-up car, singing along and banging their heads in time to the music playing on cassette. The song they are listening to is "Bohemian Rhapsody."

After the movie, "Bohemian Rhapsody" became a huge hit for a new generation of listeners. But it almost didn't happen. When writer and star Mike Myers was working on the script, the film's producer wanted to use a Guns N' Roses song instead. Myers threatened to walk off the project if anything but the Queen song was picked. Eventually, Myers won out. "I always loved 'Bohemian Rhapsody.' It was a masterpiece, and so I fought really, really hard for it," Myers said.[7]

years later, in May 2002, the hit musical *We Will Rock You* opened to sold-out audiences in London's West End. Written by Ben Elton, it uses Queen's music to tell a story about a future in which there are no musical instruments and a group of musicians fight for freedom. The show became so popular that it ran for 15 years in London and toured periodically around the world to places as far flung as Hong Kong; Zurich, Switzerland; Milan, Italy; and Auckland, New Zealand. A new iteration opened in Winnipeg, Canada, in September 2019 and toured throughout North America.

Perhaps the biggest contributor to Queen's

resurgence in popularity in the twenty-first century is the 2018 biopic *Bohemian Rhapsody*, based on Mercury's life and Queen's decades-long career as a band. Starring Rami Malek as Mercury, the movie grossed more than $51 million in box office sales in its first week alone. As of October 2019, it had made more than $900 million worldwide since it opened in theaters on November 4, 2018.[8]

> "The last 15 minutes of the show, I get to sing 'We Will Rock You,' 'We Are the Champions,' and 'Bohemian Rhapsody.' When you get to sing that trifecta of musical genius, it is very fulfilling. You do stand there on the stage and you go, 'Wow, I feel like a star.'"[9]
>
> *– Trevor Coll, star of* We Will Rock You

Bohemian Rhapsody earned Malek a Golden Globe and an Academy Award for Best Actor. It also won Academy Awards for Film Editing, Best Sound Mixing, and Best Sound Editing, as well as the Golden Globe for Best Motion Picture, Drama. But the biggest-selling biopic ever is not without its controversies. In fact, many critics insist the film is not only overrated but disrespectful to Mercury's legacy because it glosses over issues regarding his sexuality. "The film's reluctance to deal with Mercury's sexuality is catastrophic because his sexuality is so connected to the art of Queen that the two cannot be separated out," film critic Sheila O'Malley writes on RogerEbert.com. "Refusing to acknowledge queerness as an artistic force—indeed, to point at it and suggest that this is where Mercury went astray—is a deep disservice to Mercury, to Queen, to Queen fans, and to potential Queen fans."[10]

Even with these criticisms, the movie's box office success points not only to Mercury's influence on generations of fans and musicians alike but also to Queen's everlasting impact as a band. They weren't just a rock group that played in the 1980s and had a few hits. They are one of the most beloved bands of all time.

Bohemian Rhapsody versus Real Life

Though *Bohemian Rhapsody* tries to mirror Mercury's life and Queen's trajectory as a band, there are many major discrepancies between the two. Contrary to the film's claims, Mercury didn't meet Austin the same night he joined the band. John Deacon wasn't Queen's original bassist—he was the band's fourth when it hired him in 1971. Ray Foster's character in the movie—a cantankerous record executive—didn't exist in real life. Mercury's real-life boyfriend Jim Hutton didn't begin as his servant, as suggested in the movie. Mercury didn't know he was HIV positive before Live Aid. Perhaps most egregiously, Queen didn't break up just before that concert either. In fact, it never really broke up at all until after Mercury died.

Rami Malek recreated Mercury's Live Aid performance for the movie *Bohemian Rhapsody*.

CHAMPIONS OF ROCK

Since Queen's origins as Smile in the late 1960s, the band still stands as one of the greatest rock outfits the world has ever seen. Two of its original members—Taylor and May—have gone back on the road over the years, first in 2005 and 2008 with singer Paul Rodgers, who performed Mercury's parts. The trio released three records—*Return of the Champions*, a double live album, in 2005; *The Cosmos Rocks*, a studio album of new songs released in 2008; and the double live album *Live in Ukraine* in 2009. In 2012, Taylor and May linked up with *American Idol* finalist Adam Lambert and

Queen performed with Adam Lambert in Hungary in 2017.

toured as Queen + Adam Lambert. The band's music is still in heavy rotation on classic rock radio. Queen even has its own star on the Hollywood Walk of Fame in Los Angeles, California, joining the Beatles as one of the only non-American music groups to receive the honor.

For his bandmates and millions of fans the world over, Mercury's death was a tragedy. But his—and

Queen's—legacy will continue to live on in the years to come. Perhaps the lyrics to "These Are the Days of Our Lives," written for Mercury by Taylor, best sum up not only Queen's experience as a band but also its enduring message to the world: "Those days are all gone now, but one thing's still true / When I look and I find I still love you. . . . I still love you."[11]

TIMELINE

1964
Farrokh "Freddie" Bulsara and his family emigrate from Zanzibar to England.

1966
Bulsara enrolls in Ealing College and meets Tim Staffell.

1968
Brian May and Staffell form Smile, the precursor to Queen; Roger Taylor joins soon after as drummer.

1969
Bulsara meets Mary Austin and they start dating; Smile records a single for Mercury Records.

1970
Staffell leaves Smile; Bulsara replaces him; May, Taylor, and Bulsara form a new band.

1971
May, Taylor, and Bulsara hire John Deacon to play bass; they decide to call their band Queen; Bulsara changes his name to Freddie Mercury.

1973
Queen releases its first album, *Queen*, on July 13; Mercury asks Austin to marry him, but it never ends up happening.

1974
Queen's second album, *Queen II*, is released; the band tours the United States for the first time; Queen goes on tour as a headline act after *Sheer Heart Attack* is released in November, taking on Europe and Japan.

1975
Queen releases *A Night at the Opera*; "Bohemian Rhapsody" becomes the band's first Number 1 single in the United Kingdom and hits the US Top 10.

1976
A Day at the Races is released; Mercury and Austin break up.

1980

The Game is considered to be the peak of the band's commercial career; by the end of the year, Queen has sold more than 45 million albums worldwide.

1981

Queen performs in front of more than 250,000 people in São Paulo, Brazil—the largest paying audience for any band anywhere in the world at the time.

1984

Queen plays in South Africa during the apartheid era and is criticized for this decision.

1985

Queen performs at Live Aid in London's Wembley Stadium; Mercury releases his first solo album, *Mr. Bad Guy*; Mercury meets and starts dating Jim Hutton.

1987

Mercury finds out he is HIV positive but doesn't tell the band.

1989

Queen releases *The Miracle*; Mercury tells his bandmates he has AIDS, and they immediately go into the studio to record another album.

1991

Innuendo, Queen's final album as a foursome, is released on February 5; on November 23, Mercury tells the world he has AIDS in an official statement, and the next day, he dies at age 45.

1992

The Freddie Mercury Tribute Concert for AIDS Awareness is held on April 20; Queen disbands for 13 years.

2005

May and Taylor go back on tour as Queen with Paul Rodgers.

2012

May and Taylor go back on tour with *American Idol* finalist Adam Lambert.

ESSENTIAL FACTS

Queen Band Members

- **Farrokh Bulsara**, also known as **Freddie Mercury**, sang lead vocals for Queen from 1970 to 1991. He also played piano on some of the tracks and wrote many of the band's songs, such as "Bohemian Rhapsody."
- **Brian May** played lead guitar and sang back-up and sometimes lead vocals. He also wrote some of the music. He still tours periodically with Queen.
- **Roger Taylor** played the drums, sang back-up and sometimes lead vocals, and wrote some of the music. He still tours with Queen from time to time.
- **John Deacon** played bass guitar for Queen from 1971 to 1997. He also wrote some of the music, including "Another One Bites the Dust."

Queen Studio Albums

- *Queen* (1973)
- *Queen II* (1974)
- *Sheer Heart Attack* (1974)
- *A Night at the Opera* (1975)
- *A Day at the Races* (1976)
- *News of the World* (1977)
- *Jazz* (1978)
- *The Game* (1980)
- *Flash Gordon (Original Motion Picture Soundtrack)* (1980)
- *Hot Space* (1982)
- *The Works* (1984)
- *A Kind of Magic* (1986)
- *The Miracle* (1989)
- *Innuendo* (1991)
- *Made in Heaven* (1995)

Career Highlights

Queen is often called the greatest band that ever performed. The set at Live Aid on July 13, 1985, is considered one of the most legendary in rock history. The band had two Number 1 hits on the *Billboard* Top 100 Chart, "Another One Bites the Dust" and "Crazy Little Thing Called Love." Four of its songs ranked in *Billboard*'s Top 10. As of 2019, "Bohemian Rhapsody" is the third-best-selling single of all time in the United Kingdom. In 2005, Queen was crowned the most popular UK band in rock history. When the Queen biopic *Bohemian Rhapsody* came out in 2018, it earned more than $900 million in box office sales in the first six months. The movie also won four Academy Awards: Best Actor, Best Film Editing, Best Sound Editing, and Best Sound Mixing.

Conflicts

As a band, Queen didn't have a lot of conflicts, at least between its members. Queen's bandmates got along quite well and never actually broke up. But the press often ridiculed Freddie Mercury's antics on stage and the way he dressed at concerts. They also hounded him constantly about who he was dating, the nature of his sexuality, and whether he was HIV positive. Despite feeling like he was always under a microscope, Mercury never felt judged by his bandmates or his closest friends. They and many of his fans stood by him until his death in 1991.

Quote

"I won't be a rock star. I will be a legend."

—Freddie Mercury

GLOSSARY

abridged
Shortened in length.

bisexual
A person who is attracted to others of the same gender and of a different gender.

conjecture
An opinion or judgement based on little or no evidence.

debut
The first appearance, often of an album or publication, made by a musician or group.

derivative
Something that is based on another source.

encapsulate
To summarize or represent in a condensed form.

flamboyant
Attracting attention because of outlandish or exotic behavior or style.

front man
The leader in a band, usually the singer.

hypodermic needle
A medical tool with a long, thin needle often used to insert liquid drugs underneath the skin.

imperious
Domineering, overly powerful, or very snotty.

insurmountable
Unable to get over or overcome.

lavish
Very rich or fancy.

LP
An abbreviation for "long-playing record" in the music business; it's a full-length album.

monotheistic
Believing that there is only one God.

New Wave
A style of rock music popularized in the late 1970s and 1980s, especially by bands from England.

phenomenon
A very big deal.

platinum
An album is certified platinum when it sells a million units.

pleather
A plastic fabric made to look like real leather.

posthumous
Happening after someone's death.

promiscuity
The attribute of having sex with a lot of different people.

reverberated
When a loud noise or beat repeats and echoes around an area.

skiffle
A kind of folk music with a blues or jazz influence, played by a small group, that often used improvised musical instruments, such as washboards.

ADDITIONAL RESOURCES

Selected Bibliography

"About Queen." *Queen Official Site*, n.d., queenonline.com. Accessed 15 Sept. 2019.

Gilmore, Mikal. "Queen's Tragic Rhapsody." *Rolling Stone*, 7 July 2014, rollingstone.com. Accessed 15 Sept. 2019.

Hince, Peter. *Queen Unseen: My Life with the Greatest Rock Band of the 20th Century*. Music, 2015.

Jones, Lesley-Ann. *Mercury: An Intimate Biography of Freddie Mercury*. Simon, 2011.

Further Readings

Bausum, Ann. *VIRAL: The Fight against AIDS in America*. Viking, 2019.

Turn It Up! A Pitch-Perfect History of Music That Rocked the World. National Geographic Kids, 2019.

Online Resources

To learn more about Queen, please visit **abdobooklinks.com** or scan this QR code. These links are routinely monitored and updated to provide the most current information available.

More Information

For more information on this subject, contact or visit the following organizations:

Queen Studio Experience
Casino Barrière de Montreux
Rue du Théâtre 9, 1820
Montreux, Switzerland
mercuryphoenixtrust.com/studioexperience

Queen recorded seven albums at Mountain Studios in Montreux, including the final album with Mercury, *Made in Heaven*. The walk-through exhibit charts the band's association with the studios, its personal relationship with the Swiss town, and the albums that were written and recorded there. The control room has not been changed since the days when Queen worked there.

Rock & Roll Hall of Fame
1100 Rock and Roll Blvd.
Cleveland, OH 44114
216-781-7625
rockhall.com

Founded in 1995, this museum and legendary institution celebrates the people, events, and songs that have shaped rock history. Visitors can view rotating exhibits, participate in innovative educational programs, and see concerts by some of rock's most legendary artists. Every year, the museum stages a ceremony to celebrate the latest and greatest rock hall of famers.

SOURCE NOTES

CHAPTER 1. "THE WORLD'S GREATEST ROCK GIG"

1. "'Live Aid' Concert Raises $127 Million for Famine Relief in Africa." *History*, 27 July 2019, history.com. Accessed 20 Dec. 2019.

2. "Queen at Live Aid: The Real Story of How One Band Made Rock History." *Classic Rock*, 12 Nov. 2018, loudersound.com. Accessed 20 Dec. 2019.

3. "'Live Aid' Concert Raises $127 Million for Famine Relief in Africa."

4. Wesley Morris. "When Queen Took 'Bohemian Rhapsody' to Live Aid." *New York Times*, 10 Nov. 2018, nytimes.com. Accessed 20 Dec. 2019.

5. Gavin Edwards. "U2's 'Bad' Break: 12 Minutes at Live Aid That Made the Band's Career." *Rolling Stone*, 10 July 2014, rollingstone.com. Accessed 20 Dec. 2019.

6. Martin Chilton. "Queen's Live Aid Performance: How Rock's Royalty Stole the Show." *U Discover Music*, 13 July 2019, udiscovermusic.com. Accessed 20 Dec. 2019.

7. "'Live Aid' Concert Raises $127 Million for Famine Relief in Africa."

8. Chilton, "Queen's Live Aid Performance."

9. Chilton, "Queen's Live Aid Performance."

10. Morris, "When Queen Took 'Bohemian Rhapsody' to Live Aid."

11. Chilton, "Queen's Live Aid Performance."

12. Chilton, "Queen's Live Aid Performance."

13. "Queen Win Greatest Live Gig Poll." *BBC News*, 9 Nov. 2005, news.bbc.co.uk. Accessed 20 Dec. 2019.

14. Seán O'Hagan. *Freddie Mercury, The Great Pretender: A Life in Pictures.* Insight Editions, 2012. 50.

CHAPTER 2. A RAGTAG GROUP OF LONDON MUSICIANS

1. "Queen." *Rock & Roll Hall of Fame*, n.d., rockhall.com. Accessed 20 Dec. 2019.

2. Mikal Gilmore. "Queen's Tragic Rhapsody." *Rolling Stone*, 7 July 2014, rollingstone.com. Accessed 20 Dec. 2019.

3. Martin Kielty. "How Come Freddie Mercury Never Fixed His Teeth?" *Ultimate Classic Rock*, 28 Oct. 2018, ultimateclassicrock.com. Accessed 20 Dec. 2019.

4. Matt Miller. "The True Story of How Freddie Mercury Joined Queen, According to the Band's Original Singer." *Esquire*, 20 Feb. 2019, esquire.com. Accessed 20 Dec. 2019.

5. Martin Kielty. "Freddie Mercury Predecessor Has No Hard Feelings Over 'Bohemian Rhapsody' Fictionalization." *Ultimate Classic Rock*, 25 Feb. 2019, ultimateclassicrock.com. Accessed 20 Dec. 2019.

CHAPTER 3. THE BIRTH OF QUEEN

1. Mikal Gilmore. "Queen's Tragic Rhapsody." *Rolling Stone*, 7 July 2014, rollingstone.com. Accessed 20 Dec. 2019.

2. Matt Miller. "The True Story of How Freddie Mercury Joined Queen, According to the Band's Original Singer." *Esquire*, 20 Feb. 2019, esquire.com. Accessed 20 Dec. 2019.

3. "John Deacon." *Queen*, 2019, queenonline.com. Accessed 20 Dec. 2019.

4. Gilmore, "Queen's Tragic Rhapsody."

5. Gilmore, "Queen's Tragic Rhapsody."
6. Stefan Kyriazis. "Bohemian Rhapsody: Queen Crest Hidden Meaning Explained—Guess Who Designed It?" *Express*, 12 Mar. 2019, express.co.uk. Accessed 20 Dec. 2019.
7. Dominique Leone. "This Ambitious Set of Reissues Highlights a Strange Band Whose Career Was as Varied and Resourceful as Any Act in Rock." *Pitchfork*, 24 Mar. 2011, pitchfork.com. Accessed 20 Dec. 2019.

CHAPTER 4. *SHEER HEART ATTACK*

1. David Wigg. "I Was Cursed by Freddie's Fortune: Queen Star's Lover Got His Millions, Was Cruelly Attacked by Jealous Rivals and Even Abandoned by Mercury's Own Band Mates." *Daily Mail*, 30 Mar. 2013, dailymail.co.uk. Accessed 20 Dec. 2019.
2. David Wigg. "The Ex-Lover of Freddie Mercury Mary Austin Shares Her Memories of the Late Queen Singer Inside His Home." *OK! Magazine*, 17 Mar. 2000, freddie.ru. Accessed 20 Dec. 2019.
3. Wigg, "I Was Cursed by Freddie's Fortune."
4. Dana Schuster. "Meet the Woman a Closeted Freddie Mercury Fell in Love with." *New York Post*, 28 Oct. 2018, nypost.com. Accessed 20 Dec. 2019.
5. Jeff Giles. "45 Years Ago: Queen Release Second Album, 'Queen II.'" *Ultimate Classic Rock*, 8 Mar. 2016, ultimateclassicrock.com. Accessed 20 Dec. 2019.
6. Del James. "Axl Rose: The Rolling Stone Interview." *Rolling Stone*, 10 Aug. 1989, rollingstone.com. Accessed 20 Dec. 2019.
7. Max Bell. "Sheer Heart Attack: A Killer Success for Queen." *U Discover Music*, 12 July 2017, udiscovermusic.com. Accessed 20 Dec. 2019.
8. Mikal Gilmore. "Queen's Tragic Rhapsody." *Rolling Stone*, 7 July 2014, rollingstone.com. Accessed 20 Dec. 2019.
9. Stuart Kemp. "The Beatles Top the U.K.'s All-Time Sales Chart." *The Hollywood Reporter*, 5 Nov. 2012, hollywoodreporter.com. Accessed 20 Dec. 2019.
10. Kemp, "The Beatles Top the U.K.'s All-Time Sales Chart."

CHAPTER 5. TROUBLE IN PARADISE

1. Martin Kielty. "Freddie Mercury Predecessor Has No Hard Feelings Over 'Bohemian Rhapsody' Fictionalization." *Ultimate Classic Rock*, 25 Feb. 2019, ultimateclassicrock.com. Accessed 20 Dec. 2019.
2. "Queen Play Hyde Park." *BBC*, n.d., bbc.co.uk. Accessed 20 Dec. 2019.
3. "About Queen." *Queen*, 2019, queenonline.com. Accessed 20 Dec. 2019.
4. Max Bell. "'A Day at the Races': How Queen Scored Pole Position." *U Discover Music*, 10 Dec. 2019, udiscovermusic.com. Accessed 20 Dec. 2019.
5. David Wigg. "The Ex-Lover of Freddie Mercury Mary Austin Shares Her Memories of the Late Queen Singer Inside His Home." *OK! Magazine*, 17 Mar. 2000, freddie.ru. Accessed 20 Dec. 2019.
6. Yohana Desta. "Bohemian Rhapsody: The True Story Behind Freddie Mercury's Relationships." *Vanity Fair*, 1 Nov. 2018, vanityfair.com. Accessed 20 Dec. 2019.

SOURCE NOTES CONTINUED

7. David Wigg. "I Was Cursed by Freddie's Fortune: Queen Star's Lover Got His Millions, Was Cruelly Attacked by Jealous Rivals and Even Abandoned by Mercury's Own Band Mates." *Daily Mail*, 30 Mar. 2013, dailymail.co.uk. Accessed 20 Dec. 2019.

8. Wigg, "I Was Cursed by Freddie's Fortune."

9. Stephen Daw. "Freddie Mercury & Bisexuality: Why 'Bohemian Rhapsody' Struggled to Tell the Rocker's True Story." *Billboard*, 7 Nov. 2018, billboard.com. Accessed 20 Dec. 2019.

CHAPTER 6. "WE WILL ROCK YOU"

1. "Madison Square Garden." *NY Facts*, 2019, nyfacts.com. Accessed 20 Dec. 2019.

2. Robyn Dunford. *Bohemian Rhapsodies: True and Authorized Tales by Queen Fans & Celebrities.* Music Square Media, 2011. 47.

3. Dunford, *Bohemian Rhapsodies*, 47.

4. Gil Kaufman. "Queen's 'We Will Rock You/We Are The Champions' 40 Years Later: A History of the Biggest Jock Jam Single of All Time." *Billboard*, 22 Sept. 2017, billboard.com. Accessed 20 Dec. 2019.

5. Roisin O'Connor. "Freddie Mercury's Isolated Vocals on 'We Are the Champions' Will Haunt You Forever." *Independent*, 24 Nov. 2016, independent.co.uk. Accessed 20 Dec. 2019.

6. "About Queen." *Queen*, 2019, queenonline.com. Accessed 20 Dec. 2019.

7. Dunford, *Bohemian Rhapsodies*, 78.

8. Mark Blake. "How Queen Helped Tear Down the Iron Curtain." *Classic Rock*, 27 July 2016, loudersound.com. Accessed 20 Dec. 2019.

9. Dunford, *Bohemian Rhapsodies*, 78.

10. Marcos Hassan. "Remembering Queen's Infamous and History-Making Tour of South America." *Remezcla*, 21 Nov. 2018, remezcla.com. Accessed 20 Dec. 2019.

11. Mikal Gilmore. "Queen's Tragic Rhapsody." *Rolling Stone*, 7 July 2014, rollingstone.com. Accessed 20 Dec. 2019.

12. Stephen Daw. "Billy Gilman to Perform National Anthem at Angelica Ross-Hosted LGBTQ Presidential Forum." *Billboard*, 16 Sept. 2019, billboard.com. Accessed 20 Dec. 2019.

13. Paul Goodman. "Freddie Mercury's Final Performance with Queen, Knebworth Park, 1986." *Spinditty*, 6 Nov. 2019, spinditty.com. Accessed 20 Dec. 2019.

CHAPTER 7. THE LOSS OF A ROCK ICON

1. Tim Teeman. "Keep Sex, AIDS, and the Closet in Freddie Mercury's Biopic." *Daily Beast*, 16 Nov. 2018, thedailybeast.com. Accessed 20 Dec. 2019.

2. Mikal Gilmore. "Queen's Tragic Rhapsody." *Rolling Stone*, 7 July 2014, rollingstone.com. Accessed 20 Dec. 2019.

3. Tim Teeman. "I Couldn't Bear to See Freddie Wasting Away." *Tim Teeman*, 7 Sept. 2006, timteeman.com. Accessed 20 Dec. 2019.

4. Gilmore, "Queen's Tragic Rhapsody."
5. "U.S. Statistics." *HIV.gov*, 13 Mar. 2019, hiv.gov. Accessed 20 Dec. 2019.
6. Gilmore, "Queen's Tragic Rhapsody."
7. Cole Moreton. "Inside the Studio Where Freddie Mercury Sang His Last Song." *Telegraph*, 1 Dec. 2013, telegraph.co.uk. Accessed 20 Dec. 2019.
8. Moreton, "Inside the Studio."
9. Gilmore, "Queen's Tragic Rhapsody."
10. Gilmore, "Queen's Tragic Rhapsody."
11. Ron Hart. "Queen's 'Innuendo': Remembering Freddie Mercury's Last Masterpiece." *Rolling Stone*, 5 Feb. 2016, rollingstone.com. Accessed 6 Jan. 2020.
12. David Wigg. "The Ex-Lover of Freddie Mercury Mary Austin Shares Her Memories of the Late Queen Singer Inside His Home." *OK! Magazine*, 17 Mar. 2000, freddie.ru. Accessed 20 Dec. 2019.
13. David Wigg. "I Was Cursed by Freddie's Fortune: Queen Star's Lover Got His Millions, Was Cruelly Attacked by Jealous Rivals and Even Abandoned by Mercury's Own Band Mates." *Daily Mail*, 30 Mar. 2013, dailymail.co.uk. Accessed 20 Dec. 2019.

CHAPTER 8. QUEEN'S LEGACY

1. "The Largest Farewell: The Freddie Mercury Tribute Concert 25 Years Ago." *DW*, 19 Apr. 2017, dw.com. Accessed 20 Dec. 2019.
2. "The Largest Farewell."
3. "The Largest Farewell."
4. "About the MPT." *The Mercury Phoenix Trust*, n.d., mercuryphoenixtrust.com. Accessed 20 Dec. 2019.
5. Mikal Gilmore. "Queen's Tragic Rhapsody." *Rolling Stone*, 7 July 2014, rollingstone.com. Accessed 20 Dec. 2019.
6. Cole Moreton. "Inside the Studio Where Freddie Mercury Sang His Last Song." *Telegraph*, 1 Dec. 2013, telegraph.co.uk. Accessed 20 Dec. 2019.
7. Elahe Izadi. "Scaramouche! The Story of How 'Bohemian Rhapsody' Ended up in 'Wayne's World' And Became a Phenomenon Again." *Washington Post*, 2 Nov. 2018, washingtonpost.com. Accessed 20 Dec. 2019.
8. "Bohemian Rhapsody." *IMDb*, 2019, imdb.com. Accessed 20 Dec. 2019.
9. David Chiu. "Fresh Off 'Bohemian Rhapsody,' Queen Musical 'We Will Rock You' Tours North America." *Forbes*, 2 Sept. 2019, forbes.com. Accessed 20 Dec. 2019.
10. Sheila O'Malley. "Bohemian Rhapsody." *Roger Ebert*, 2 Nov. 2018, rogerebert.com. Accessed 20 Dec. 2019.
11. "These Are the Days of Our Lives." *Genius*, 2019, genius.com. Accessed 20 Dec. 2019.

INDEX

ABOUT THE AUTHOR

Alexis Burling

Alexis Burling has written dozens of articles and books for young readers on a variety of topics, such as current events, famous people, nutrition and fitness, careers and money management, relationships, and cooking. She is also a book critic with reviews of both adult and young adult books, author interviews, and other industry-related articles published in the *New York Times*, *Washington Post*, *San Francisco Chronicle*, and more. Burling lives in Portland, Oregon, with her husband. She has fond memories of listening to Queen when she was growing up during the 1970s and 1980s.